Join the
Band

by Pippa Goodhart

Illustrated by Andy Rowland

Notes on the series

TIDDLERS are structured to provide support for children who are starting to read on their own. The stories may also be used for sharing with children.

Starting to read alone can be daunting. **TIDDLERS** help by listing the words in the book for a check before reading, and by providing visual support and repeating words and phrases. These books will both develop confidence and encourage reading and rereading for pleasure.

If you are reading this book with a child, here are a few suggestions:

1. Make reading fun! Choose a time to read when you and the child are relaxed and have time to share the story.
2. Talk about the story before you start reading. Look at the cover and the blurb. What might the story be about? Why might the child like it?
3. Look also at the list of words below - can the child tackle most of the words?
4. Encourage the child to retell the story, using the jumbled picture puzzle.
5. Give praise! Remember that small mistakes need not always be corrected.

Here is a list of the words in this story.

Common words:

and	I	said
bird	in	stop
can	is	the
cat	new	was
dog	no	went
here	rabbit	

Other words:

band	join	twang
boom	played	tweet
drum	sad	until
howl	ting	wag

Here is the band.

"Twang, twang,"
went Cat.

"Ting, ting,"
went Rabbit.

7

"Tweet, tweet," went Bird.

"Howl!" went Dog.
"Can I join in?"

"No!" said Rabbit
and Bird.

"Stop!" said Cat.

Dog was sad ...

15

... until the
band played.

Wag, wag,
went Dog.

"Boom, boom!"
went the drum.

Here is the new band.

Puzzle Time

Can you find these pictures in the story?

Which pages are the
pictures from?

Turn over for answers!

Answers

The pictures come from these pages:

a. pages 14–15

b. pages 8–9

c. pages 18–19

d. pages 16–17

First published in 2014 by
Franklin Watts
338 Euston Road
London
NW1 3BH

Franklin Watts Australia
Level 17/207 Kent Street
Sydney
NSW 2000

Text © Pippa Goodhart 2014
Illustration © Andy Rowland 2014

The rights of Pippa Goodhart to be
identified as the author and Andy Rowland
as the illustrator of this Work have been
asserted in accordance with the Copyright,
Designs and Patents Act, 1988.

A CIP catalogue record for this book is
available from the British Library.

ISBN 978 1 4451 3270 9 (hbk)
ISBN 978 1 4451 3272 3 (pbk)
ISBN 978 1 4451 3269 3 (ebook)
ISBN 978 1 4451 3271 6 (library ebook)

Series Editor: Jackie Hamley
Editor: Melanie Palmer
Series Advisor: Catherine Glavina
Series Designer: Peter Scoulding

Printed in China

Franklin Watts is a division of Hachette Children's Books,
an Hachette UK company. www.hachette.co.uk